NO EXIT

Janice Green

SADDLEBACK
EDUCATIONAL PUBLISHING

QREADS

SADDLEBACK
EDUCATIONAL PUBLISHING
www.sdlback.com

ISBN-13: 978-1-61651-202-6
ISBN-10: 1-61651-202-4
eBook: 978-1-60291-924-2

Printed in the U.S.A.

20 19 18 17 16   5 6 7 8 9

■ ■ ■

Kimo looked around. Earlier, he'd seen someone who looked like a security guard. But now the guy was out of sight. Kimo stared at the rack of cool, expensive belts in front of him. He reached for one as he pulled out the elastic waistband of his sweat pants. He let the length of the belt drop down the inside of his pantleg. The belt buckle stuck out, held up by the elastic, but it was hidden by his jacket.

He looked around again. Now the security guard was there—right there—staring at him. Kimo froze. But what was this? Instead of moving in on him, the security guy *smiled*.

Kimo couldn't believe it. He walked away

quickly, before the guy changed his mind. Besides the belt, Kimo had a ring, a wallet, and a watch hidden in his jacket. It was time to leave the mall.

He walked toward the south exit of Lane's department store, the one nearest the bus stop. Another security guard was there, standing right next to the exit. He turned back into the mall. He walked past Computer Planet, Touchstone Books, Candy Land, and Electronics Unlimited. He paused in front of a new SUV, which was first prize in a drawing. Frowning, he pretended to read the contest rules. A crowd of people were streaming out the main exit. As he tried to blend in, he saw two security guards, a man and woman, stationed at both sides of the exit.

Tension tightened the back of Kimo's neck. He went back into Lane's, weaving in and out of the clothing displays. It was nearly dinnertime; the crowd of shoppers was thinning out.

When no one was watching, he headed

to another exit from Lane's and joined the crowd leaving the store. He heaved a sigh of relief as he pushed open the door. Outside, he felt a heavy blast of heat from the humid summer night.

■ ■ ■

Then suddenly, a hand fell on his shoulder—a strong, hard hand.

"Security," a man said quietly as he gripped Kimo's arm.

"Come with us, please." Kimo looked around. Another guard was on his left.

Anger and frustration rose in his chest—but he knew better than to run. One time he'd done that at another mall. Three security guards had chased him into a dumpster. When they caught him, they'd broken two of his fingers before dragging him back to the store.

These two guys were smooth. The people around them didn't notice what was going on when Kimo was led back into Lane's. The men took him to the top floor. All around the huge room, rolls of carpet lay in neat stacks. The guards walked Kimo up to what looked like a blank, white wall. Then one of them turned a white handle, and a door opened inward.

Kimo was led down a dim hallway to a large office. A thick carpet with intricate patterns was spread out on the floor. Soft yellow lights made the walls glow as if the room was lit by candles. A handsome man sat behind an enormous desk. His expression was kind and mild. When he spoke, Kimo felt a shiver run down his spine. The man's voice was deep and dark and full. It seemed to vibrate through Kimo's head.

"Come in, son. My name is Dieous," he said. "Security says you have a belt, a ring, a wallet, and a watch. Let me see them, please."

As if hypnotized, Kimo obeyed, laying the stolen goods on the polished surface of the desktop.

Dieous fingered the ring. "That's quite a diamond," he said. "How did you manage this? Tell me your secret."

"I asked the clerk to show me the rings," Kimo mumbled. "When he put them on the counter, I asked about another item—so he'd have to look away. That's when I switched the fake diamond ring for the real one."

"I imagine you're very fast," said Dieous. "And this watch—it's the most expensive one we sell. You used the same method?"

Kimo nodded.

Dieous pushed the items across the desktop. He smiled at Kimo and said, "They're yours."

Kimo gaped at him. Dieous smiled and turned to a young guy about Kimo's age who was standing nearby. Kimo hadn't noticed him before.

"Bobby," Dieous said, "take this boy shopping."

■ ■ ■

Nodding, Bobby took Kimo downstairs to the men's department. "What is this?" Kimo asked him. "What's going on?"

"Don't worry about it," Bobby said. "Dieous

likes you. You're set."

"Set for what?" Kimo asked.

"You like these jackets?" Bobby asked.

Kimo nodded. He'd never even tried to steal a jacket as nice as these!

"Why don't you try one on?" Bobby suggested. "Go ahead."

Forty minutes later, Kimo was wearing all new clothes. "Tight threads," Bobby said. "You got good taste, buddy."

"I can't believe I get to keep these," Kimo said uncertainly.

"Dieous owns this mall," Bobby said with a shrug. "He's generous."

"But what does he want from me?" Kimo asked suspiciously.

"He just wants you to stick around. You getting hungry yet?" Bobby asked, as he headed toward the food court.

Kimo frowned. "What do you mean 'stick around'? Maybe I don't want to."

Bobby raised an eyebrow. "You got some place you'd rather be?" he said.

Kimo thought of the streets where he

usually hung out. Just last week a guy there had held a knife to his neck and robbed him. No—right now there was no place he'd rather be.

At the food court, Bobby told Kimo to order anything he wanted. Kimo had a steak. Two young women walked by, and Kimo could tell they were checking him out. He felt great. "Can I have another steak?" he asked.

Bobby laughed. "Pretty soon you'll stop asking," he said. "Come on, let's go. He'll be waiting for us."

■ ■ ■

Dieous smiled as Kimo came into his office. He motioned for Kimo to sit down next to his large desk.

"Uh—could you tell me what this is all about now?" Kimo asked nervously.

Dieous put his long fingers together and leaned close to Kimo. "Indeed I can. This place is about protection and belonging— happiness that you never thought was possible." His voice wasn't loud, but it filled the room. "Here with me," he went on, "you're free from danger—from those who would wound your very soul. Here, there are no bad influences to lead you down a path that can only end in prison or death."

Dieous smiled. "You've had enough of the cold and uncaring world, the hungry child and the bare cupboard—haven't you? You're free from the homeless woman who can hardly walk because of the festering sores on her feet. The filthy rats that squeal and fight over the garbage in our streets. *Free!* Here, you can leave all that behind and join us in true happiness."

Dieous' eyes glowed with excitement. As the man's voice vibrated in Kimo's head, he felt as if he were sitting inside a big bass fiddle. When Dieous stopped talking, Kimo was exhausted. But he felt happy and—*saved*.

Then Dieous led him to a room behind his office. It was a sort of dormitory, but much nicer—with thick carpets and real beds. Kimo had slept in a box when he was a baby, and then a mattress on the floor. Some other guys, all about his age, were stretched out on the beds. Dieous pointed to an empty bed and handed him a Walkman and headphones. "Listen before you sleep," he said. "You'll learn all about us."

Kimo lay down and turned on the tape. It was Dieous explaining how he'd lost his own two sons to drugs and prison. After their deaths, he said, he had dedicated his life to rescuing young people—to building a family whose safety he could guarantee.

When he'd heard the whole tape, Kimo stretched out and immediately fell into a deep, peaceful sleep. It was the first time in years Kimo slept without watching his back.

■ ■ ■

An hour later, Bobby shook Kimo's shoulder until he woke up.

"Huh? What time is it?" Kimo asked in a groggy voice.

"It's 10:00 P.M.—closing time. When all the outsiders leave the mall, the place is ours!"

Bobby said with a wink.

"Have I been asleep that long?" Kimo asked.

"You sure have. Now we've got to go to Lane's," said Bobby.

"Again?" Kimo asked.

"Get new clothes, man," Bobby said. "We got a wedding rehearsal tonight."

"Yeah, right. Who's getting married—you?" Kimo teased.

"No!" Bobby said harshly.

"Hey, chill, man! I didn't know. I'm new here, remember?" said Kimo.

"Sorry," said Bobby. "Let's get some food and then head for Lane's."

An hour later, Kimo was dressed in a beautiful pearl-gray suit. "What do you think?" he asked Bobby. "Is it better than the black one?"

"Ten times better," Bobby said.

"No, it's a hundred times better!" a female voice chimed in.

Bobby laughed. "Hey!" he yelled. "Come on out, Rasheeda!"

Two young women came out from behind a pillar. One was tall, with a lively face and a broad smile. The other had a sweet, sad expression. Her slightly tilted eyes never left Bobby's face.

"This is Tiffany," Bobby said quietly. His hand reached out hesitantly—as if he wanted to touch her.

"And I'm Rasheeda," said the tall young woman. "Are you an eighteen or a twenty-one?"

"Huh?" said Kimo.

"Those were the ages of Dieous' kids when they died," Rasheeda said. "Everybody here is either eighteen or twenty-one. Which one are you?"

"I'm twenty-one," said Kimo.

"Good! Me, too," Rasheeda said. "So you can sit next to me at rehearsal."

"Hey, you move pretty fast, girl!" Kimo said, grinning.

"Sometimes not fast enough," Rasheeda said softly. It was then that Kimo noticed a scar that ran from her cheekbone to her neck.

He wondered if she'd been thinking about the scar when she said "not fast enough."

The rehearsal was on the top floor of Lane's, in the room with the carpets. The carpet rolls now bordered each side of a long, wide path. Tall bouquets of artificial flowers stood at each corner. Bobby told Kimo just where to stand. Before long about 20 young women and men joined them. Everyone was dressed up, looking good. Kimo felt a swell of pride that he was one of them.

At the end of the path were two tall vases of artificial flowers. A young man in a white suit walked up and stood there, waiting. He had a thin, sharp face and a smug manner.

Then someone turned on a tape deck, and music filled the room. Wearing a white suit, Dieous stepped out of his office. He was leading a young woman into the room—Tiffany! Kimo glanced at Bobby. Bobby looked as tight as the string on a violin bow.

Tiffany held Dieous' arm as he walked her up the path. His step was stately; his face glowed with pride. He led her up to the smug young man and then stood before them. When Dieous started to speak, Kimo was awed once again by the power of his voice.

"We are here today to witness and celebrate the union of Raymond and Tiffany," Dieous announced.

Kimo saw a tear trickle down Tiffany's cheek. He felt a stab of pity for her and Bobby—and he stopped listening to Dieous' voice. As he looked around at the young men and women standing there, their faces fixed on Dieous, a shiver went up his back. He was surprised to realize that Dieous' face didn't look kind anymore.

After the rehearsal, Kimo took Bobby aside. "Why are you allowing Dieous to marry her off to that Raymond guy? *You're* the one she wants," he said.

Bobby wouldn't look at him. "We're not right for each other," he said. "Dieous says so. When the time comes—"

"Hey! Just *what* does Dieous know? Everything? Is he a god or something?" Kimo demanded.

"Not so loud!" Bobby whispered. "Look, man, you don't understand. If not for Dieous, I'd be dead. We'd all be dead!"

"Not *me!*" Kimo snapped.

"Is that right?" Bobby said with heavy sarcasm. "How many times have you been arrested? Two? Three? How close are you to doing prison time?"

Kimo frowned. He was close. "But prison doesn't mean you have to *die,*" he said. "Just stay tough. Stay smart."

"Ha!" Bobby said bitterly. "Do you happen to personally know anybody who walked out of prison alive?"

Kimo's mouth twisted. Just four months ago, his cousin had been killed in prison— stabbed with a jagged piece of pipe. "Okay," he said. "Dieous is great. He's wonderful. But I'm leaving."

■ ■ ■

Slowly shaking his head, Bobby gave Kimo a long look.

"I'm getting out of here. You gonna tell security?" Kimo asked.

"I don't have to," said Bobby.

"Nice knowing you," Kimo said as he walked off, heading out into the mall.

A giant poster on a store window caught his eye. It pictured an exploding volcano. "Make your own," the caption invited. The store was called Discovery Child. "Kid stuff," Kimo thought to himself, but who cared? He went inside and opened a "Make a Volcano" kit. It contained a plastic volcano and little jars of vinegar and baking soda. He used those ingredients to "make an eruption." Then he read the booklet called "How Volcanoes Work" and moved on to a kit that promised "25 Great Experiments." He did them all.

After Discovery Child, he went into Computer Planet. He'd never used the Internet before—but people said you could find anything there. He picked up a slim book, *Beginner's Guide to the Net,* and checked it out. Soon he was online, reading about volcanoes, insects, and South America.

Hours later Kimo's stomach growled. Lightheaded with hunger, he was amazed that he'd spent so much time learning—just like a student! He'd quit school after ninth grade, hating it. But now that he thought about school, he remembered it differently. It was the gangs and the fights and the fear of being jumped in the stairwell he couldn't stand. It wasn't *learning* that he'd hated.

Kimo ate a quick meal in the food court and then decided it was time to disappear. When he was sure no one was looking, he ducked into Touchstone Books. He sat down behind a tall bookshelf near the back of the store. After reading most of a book about computers, he lay down on the carpet and dozed. About 4:00 A.M. he heard soft footsteps. He was instantly awake, straining to hear every noise. As the footsteps came near, he crawled behind a low shelf in the kids' section. The footsteps paused. It was so quiet Kimo could hear the person give a faint sigh. He wanted to take a look, but he didn't dare.

Finally, the footsteps moved off.

Kimo stayed where he was, dozing and waking. He doubted that the others were trying very hard to find him. After all, there were a thousand places to hide in the mall. They'd be smarter to wait until he tried to leave.

At 10:00 the next morning, people began to drift into the bookstore. Kimo left then, taking his time, checking out the shoppers. Soon he saw what he was looking for—a family that looked something like him. The parents seemed old enough to have a 21-year-old son. He followed them at a distance. First they went to Fast Feet to get shoes for their skinny kid who looked about 10. Then they bought a basketball for the teenage daughter at AJ Sports. Then on to Lane's. "Something for Grandma's birthday," he heard the mother say.

On the fifth floor, the mother spent a long time looking at vases, picture frames, and mirrors. Finally, she picked out a heavy-looking glass sculpture with lots of tiny colored bubbles inside.

When the sculpture was boxed and bagged, the family headed out the door. Kimo joined them, pretending to search the parking lot for the car. But then, from the corner of his eye, Kimo saw a tall man begin to move toward him—a security guard!

Kimo turned and darted back into Lane's. He swerved toward the escalator. Another guard! He grabbed a heavy flower pot and threw it wildly. When it smashed into a shelf, half a dozen picture frames scattered like bowling pins. Someone screamed.

Kimo was cornered! He charged for the door, pushing through the knot of people gathered there. The door had begun to open when a tall, heavyset guy grabbed him by both shoulders. Kimo thrashed desperately, but the muscular guy got a good hold on one arm and pinned it to his chest.

"Got him!" the guy yelled.

The guards, three of them now, came hustling through the crowd.

Kimo tried to resist. *"Help!"* he yelled. But

the hostile faces all around told him that it was useless. Who would believe him? A guard snapped handcuffs on his wrists. As Kimo was led away, a little boy glared at him and kicked his leg. Somehow, that made Kimo feel worse than anything.

■ ■ ■

It was ironic, Kimo thought as they led him through the white door. So many times he'd strolled out of a mall with his pockets stuffed with stolen goods. Now, when he was innocent, he was caught big time.

The guards led him beyond Dieous' office, beyond the dormitories, to a small, dark room with a large mirror. Kimo assumed it was a two-way mirror. Then, while one man held Kimo's arms behind his back, the other two beat him. Through a red haze of pain, Kimo wondered at the coldness of it all. Always before—when he'd hurt someone or been hurt—it had been in the heat of anger. But these three guards showed no emotion at all. When they were finished, he lay on the floor, unable to move. One of the guards bent over him and said coldly, "Get the message? Next time, you'll need a wheelchair."

A man carrying headphones and a tape came in next. "Keep it on," he said, "or the guards will be coming back."

Dieous' voice was on the tape, of course. Again he spoke in soothing tones about security and belonging. At first Kimo listened, hoping the voice would distract him from the pain. It didn't.

At last Kimo had had enough. He couldn't help rebelling against Dieous' message. "Blah, blah, blah," he whispered, mockingly. It worked! His own voice was drowning Dieous out. He didn't speak a word out loud. He didn't *dare*. But inside his head he was saying, "I'm going back to school. I'm going to get a job. I'm going back to school—"

After a while, Kimo stopped talking and started thinking. He knew he couldn't return to his old neighborhood without getting sucked back into his old life. Maybe he'd go live with his Aunt Carol. She had a nice big house 70 miles away. Carol would expect a lot of him. But maybe she was just what he needed.

■ ■ ■

The next day, Kimo stayed in bed. His body ached and it hurt to move. But his mind was racing, planning. In his old life, he'd always allowed himself to be swept along from day to day. Now he was beginning to see a future. For the first time, he felt in charge. But before that future could begin, he had to escape—and he was determined not to go alone.

He started with Rasheeda. "Come on, tell me the truth. Are you happy hanging out in this mall every day?"

"Yeah, I'm happy enough. What's wrong with it?" Rasheeda asked.

"Well, what about going outside? Don't you ever want to?" Kimo said.

Rasheeda looked at him for a long moment. "I can't make it on the outside, Kimo," she said softly.

"Are you in trouble? What'd you do out there?" Kimo asked.

"You don't want to know," Rasheeda muttered. She walked away quickly.

Next, Kimo tried Bobby.

"No way, man. I can't go out there," Bobby said. "I'll just get back on drugs again—I know it."

"Can't you get into a program? At least you could *try,*" Kimo insisted.

"I *did* try. I tried *everything*—and then I just went back," Bobby said.

Kimo was getting nowhere. But he kept on and got better at it.

He talked to Rasheeda again. "When you marry some guy Dieous picks out for you, are you gonna have kids?"

"Sure," said Rasheeda. "I guess."

"Where are your kids gonna go to school?" said Kimo.

"Dieous says *he'll* teach the kids," Rasheeda answered.

"You want your kids to grow up in *here*— where they'll never even see the sun come up?" Kimo asked.

Rasheeda frowned and looked away.

He saw one of the eighteens, a guy named Curtis, admiring the SUV. The drawing was going to be held the next weekend.

"First thing I'm gonna do when I get out is drive a car," Kimo told Curtis. "I've always wanted to do that."

He asked Tiffany, "You really want to have kids with Raymond?"

He told Bobby, "I'm leaving real soon. You and Tiffany should come."

This time Bobby looked interested. "How are you gonna do it?" he asked.

Kimo told him.

"That could work," Bobby said slowly.

"Think about it," said Kimo. "Leaving would be the best thing you ever did."

Kimo saw hope in Bobby's eyes.

■ ■ ■

When Kimo decided he was ready, eight people had agreed to come along with him. There were a few who said they couldn't leave. But all of them promised not to give him away. There were also a few that Kimo hadn't talked to—like Raymond.

The mall closed early Monday nights. So Kimo chose a Monday morning for the escape. At 5:00 A.M. he woke Curtis, Bobby, and another guy, Dwight. They crept out of the dormitory. The women were already waiting out in the carpet area. As they quietly walked through Lane's cosmetic department, Rasheeda said, "Let's take some stuff with us. I want to look good when I get out." She reached out and grabbed a lipstick.

Kimo grabbed her wrist. "No! We gotta start out clean. Otherwise, we're never gonna stay that way," he said.

Rasheeda pulled her wrist away. "Don't you order me around!" she cried.

"Come on, girl!" Tiffany said. "We don't want *nothing* that belongs to Dieous." Gently, she took the lipstick from Rasheeda's hand.

They got to the SUV, its slick, new body shining in the dim light. Kimo took a quick look around. No sign of security anywhere. He quickly went to work trying to hot-wire the engine.

Curtis bent over him. "You took care of the airbag?"

"Last night," said Kimo. "We got no airbag to worry about."

"Hey, you're *good,* man," Curtis said admiringly.

Kimo nodded grimly. He vowed this was the last thing that he'd ever steal. Then he said, "Everybody in. And *hurry!* We gotta take off real quick!"

Everyone climbed in the shiny SUV. Rasheeda, the only one who knew how to drive, was at the wheel. Kimo touched the ignition wires together. The engine sputtered, then roared to life. The sound echoed through the mall.

"Seatbelts!" Rasheeda cried out.

Kimo glanced over at her. Her long hands were tight on the steering wheel; her big brown eyes blazed with both fear and excitement. He wanted to pat her on the back, but there was no time.

"Here we go!" Bobby yelled.

The exit was just ahead, covered by a rolling metal door. Then they heard shouts. Behind them, several security guards were moving fast.

■ ■ ■

Rasheeda gunned the motor and charged the door. "Duck down!" she yelled. Kimo ducked, his arms around his head, bracing himself against the dashboard. They hit the metal door with an enormous crash. In spite of the seat belt, Kimo's arms slammed painfully against the dashboard. Then he rebounded—hard—against the seat.

Now there was a huge dent in the door, and daylight showed through the top and sides of the beautiful new SUV. The crumpled metal groaned. One more hit would do it.

Rasheeda backed up. Then, as she paused for an instant to change gears, security guards seemed to be all over the car. One guard leapt up, reaching through the window and trying to grab the steering wheel.

Rasheeda was struggling to tear the guard loose when another guard popped up on the passenger side. Kimo opened the door fast, sending the guy reeling backward. Yells and sounds of struggle came from the back seat. Another security guard appeared at the window. Kimo fought him off, while trying to punch the button to close the windows.

"Stop!" It was Dieous. He stood in front of the car, his arms partly raised. Everyone froze.

Kimo had never heard Dieous raise his voice, but now it *boomed.* "Guards!" he commanded. "Leave my children for now. Rasheeda—turn off the engine."

The guards backed away. Kimo looked at the others. Bobby looked terrified. The fire in Rasheeda's eyes had gone out. She stopped driving forward.

"Kimo, Bobby—all of you," Dieous said. "Get out of the car and come to my office. You will be punished and—"

"We're *not* your puppets! We're not your *children!"* Kimo yelled desperately, trying to drown out Dieous' voice.

Then Tiffany's voice could be heard from the back seat. She chanted, *"We're not your puppets! We're not your children!"*

Bobby joined in, followed by Curtis. Then Rasheeda. The SUV began to reverberate with their voices.

Rasheeda's face was glowing as she looked over at Kimo. She nodded and the SUV slowly moved forward. Dieous looked surprised. The ruined bumper came close to Dieous' chest. Kimo raised his fist, urging them on, and their voices rose still louder: *"We're not your puppets! We're not your children!"*

Finally, Dieous stepped aside.

"Whooooo!" Kimo yelled. "Tear it down, Rasheeda!"

She gunned the motor until it screamed. The SUV hurled forward—and with a tearing crash, the metal door shuddered and collapsed.

While her friends cheered wildly, Rasheeda drove over the door and out into the empty parking lot. The sky was pink with the coming dawn. Daylight had never looked better.

After-Reading Wrap-Up

1. Imagine you were one of the kids in the story. What would you like about living in the mall? What would you not like?

2. What were Dieous' good points? What were his bad points?

3. What event made Kimo want to leave the mall?

4. When Kimo spent time alone in the stores, what did he learn about himself?

5. Where does Kimo plan to live after leaving the mall?

6. As Kimo escapes, he vows never to go back to his old life. Do you think he'll succeed? Give at least two reasons for your opinion.